P9-AZW-385

SEP 15 2014

PROPERTY OF
BOURBONNAIS PUBLIC LIBRARY

This book is for N.

TODDLER
RAS

The art in this book was made with acrylic on paper.
The text was set in 26-point Zapatisa.

Library of Congress Cataloging-in-Publication Data

Raschka, Christopher.
Moosey Moose / Chris Raschka.
pages cm
Revised edition. Originally published by Hyperion Books for Children, 2000.
Summary: Moosey Moose wants his long pants.
ISBN 978-1-4197-1202-9
[1. Moose—Fiction.] I. Title.
PZ7.R1814Mo 2014
[E]—dc23
2013034060

Text and illustrations copyright © 2014 Chris Raschka
Book design by Meagan Bennett

Published in 2014 by Abrams Appleseed, an imprint of ABRAMS. All rights reserved. No portion of this book
may be reproduced, stored in a retrieval system, or transmitted in any form or by any means, mechanical,
electronic, photocopying, recording, or otherwise, without written permission from the publisher.

Abrams Appleseed is a registered trademark of Harry N. Abrams, Inc.

Printed and bound in China
10 9 8 7 6 5 4 3 2 1

For bulk discount inquiries, contact specialsales@abramsbooks.com.

ABRAMS
THE ART OF BOOKS SINCE 1949
115 West 18th Street
New York, NY 10011
www.abramsbooks.com

CHRIS RASCHKA

MOOSEY MOOSE

ABRAMS APPLESEED
NEW YORK

Moosey Moose is mad.

Yes, Moosey Moose
is mad!

Why? Why is Moosey Moose mad?

Moosey Moose
wants his pants.

His long pants.

Not his short pants.

Here are his long pants.

Moosey Moose!

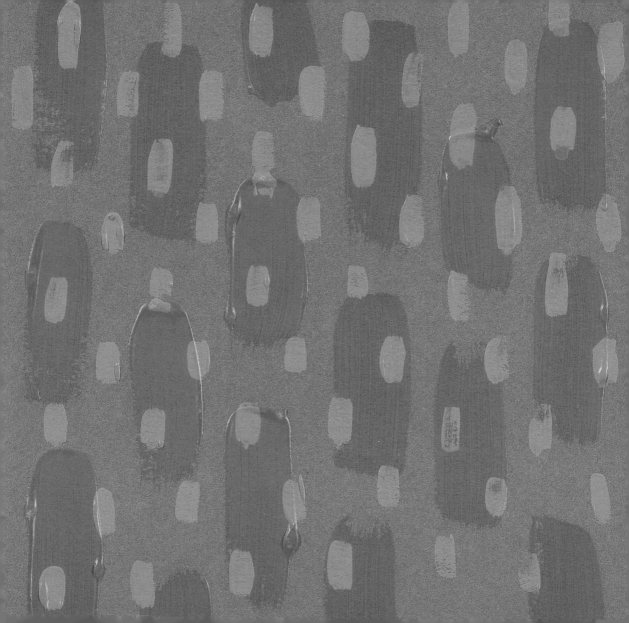